# A FISHY MURDER MOST FOUL

## A MOLLY GREY COZY MYSTERY

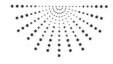

## DONNA DOYLE

Publisher's Note: This is a work of fiction. Names, characters, places, and incidents are a product of the author's imagination. Locales and public names are sometimes used for atmospheric purposes. Any resemblance to actual people, living or dead, or to businesses, companies, events, institutions, or locales is completely coincidental.

© 2021 PUREREAD LTD

# CONTENTS

# CONTENTS

1

# MY FIRST JOB AT THE CALMHAVEN SENTINEL

At first the day had started off like any other day for the past three months; boring.

A while back, I had applied for the job as a news reporter at the Calmhaven Sentinel, and they had hired me. Nobody had given me a chance. Not even my mother.

"A reporter... you?" she had said, while her eyes had been almost as wide as those shiny marbles that my little friend Jimmy and I used to play with when we were children, on the streets of Calmhaven. She shook her head in dismay and mumbled, "That's way out of your league, Virgil. Remember, we had to drag you through elementary school? Your grammar is as bad as a leaky faucet."

*Thanks, Mom. I am always glad to receive a word of encouragement.*

Mom failed to remember I had finished two online courses on creative writing, and I had done a lot of research on YouTube about journalism. None of those things had earned me a crisp diploma on parchment paper that said in golden, twirling letters that Virgil Shepherd was a trustworthy writer, and therefore the family did not believe I could write.

But I wanted to prove them wrong and had started with great hopes. I was ready to hit the big times. I dreamt about being hired by the New York Times or Newsweek and was certain my byline would one day appear in the National Geographic, as my Motorola Smartphone made nice pictures.

But Jack Stapleton, my boss and a skilled editor, believed in the good old-fashioned school of hard-knocks, and he wanted me to start at the bottom of the ladder. So I never wrote even a single paragraph in those first three months.

Mopping floors, cleaning toilets, and serving coffee with donuts to the overworked journalists on call. Old school journalistic training! Not quite my idea of being successful.

But that morning, when I heard Jack Stapleton calling out my name, his booming voice echoing through the office, things changed.

I ran over to his cubicle, the holy of holies of the Calmhaven Sentinel, and knocked on his glass door while holding my breath. What was it this time? Another computer screen that needed dusting?

"Come in, Virgil," Stapleton sang. He raked with his hand through his wavy, black hair and looked at me with those piercing blue eyes of his. "I've got a job for you."

"A job?"

He leaned back in his swivel chair, plucked at his suspenders and said, "I want you to interview Miss Molly Gertrude Grey."

For a moment, I stared at him; not sure if I had heard correctly. "You mean… an actual interview?"

Stapleton frowned. "I'll be honest with you, Virgil. I had much rather given the job to one of my more… well, experienced journalists, but everyone is busy and this is an emergency, so I have no choice but to send you."

A spurt of enthusiasm welled up in the pit of my stomach. This would be my chance, my long-awaited breakthrough. I rubbed my nose and asked, "Who is Miss Molly Gertrude Grey?"

I had never heard her name, but that didn't mean much, as I barely even read the Calmhaven Sentinel myself. But, no doubt, this woman was a celebrity. Famous or infamous. Maybe, she had won Calmhaven's beauty pageant, and they would usher me into her penthouse for an exclusive interview, complete with wine and caviar. Or, and this was just as good, the recent heist of Calmhaven's First National Bank had been her brain child, and I would talk to her in jail, surrounded by stern looking prison guards with their rifles trained, ready to fire.

"She runs a wedding agency," Stapleton replied giving me the 'It's-time-you-read-our-newspaper,' look. "It's called The Cozy Bridal Agency," and the office has been in operation for twenty-five years."

I frowned. I had just turned twenty-five myself, which meant the Cozy Bridal Agency was just about the same age. So this lady was not a beauty queen, and neither was she a notorious criminal. "How old is this woman?" I stuttered.

Stapleton shrugged his shoulders. "Does it matter?"

"Not really," I answered, feeling rather dumb.

But Stapleton was helpful. "As far as I know she's around 80 years. I want you to meet her and talk to her about her life, the Agency, and anything that is appropriate. She is quite a personality in the town and the anniversary of the Agency is of interest to the nice folks of Calmhaven."

*80 years old?* I sighed. "Will my article be on the front page, Mr. Stapleton?"

"No, Virgil," Stapleton sneered. "That page is for the real important stuff, like the present drought and the war overseas. Your article, if it is any good, comes somewhere towards the end of the paper. 300 Words, no more, you get it? I want it on my desk next Friday."

Stapleton leaned forward again, picked up a paper from his desk and began to read. Without looking up, he motioned with his hand that I was to leave the Holy of Holies. But then, just before I stepped out the door, he cleared his throat. "Oh, Virgil?"

I stopped. "Yes, Mr. Stapleton?"

"That Molly Gertrude Grey, she's a sleuth too," Stapleton answered, still not looking up. "She has solved many crimes over the years; crimes our police officer JJ Barnes couldn't even crack. It's interesting for our readers if you at least mention that aspect of her life in your article."

*An 80-year-old crime-busting grandma? Now that's more interesting!*

I nodded politely. "Thank you for the opportunity, Mr. Stapleton. I won't let you down."

But Stapleton did not seem to hear my last comment. His mind was on an article about the unwanted side effects of the facelift of Calmhaven's only movie star, and I closed the door behind me.

I had an assignment. Not a fantastic one, but it was an assignment, and I had begun to climb the ladder in my career as a journalist.

## 2

# MEETING MISS MOLLY GERTRUDE

**M**iss Molly Gertrude was most forthcoming when I called her on the phone that afternoon. She had a normal house phone. I wondered if she even had a mobile phone. After all, she was 80. It could be an interesting detail.

It took time, but at last somebody picked up and a cheerful voice greeted me. "Hello, you are talking to Molly Gertrude Grey from the Cozy Bridal Agency. How may I help you?"

Her voice reminded me of Aunt Abigail, a favorite relative of mine from my mother's side, who seemed to possess a gentle warmth that was lacking in the rest of my family.

I cleared my throat. "This is Virgil Shepherd, from the Calmhaven Sentinel, Ma'am. Our newspaper wants to do an exclusive interview with you about your work as a wedding planner."

It was silent for a few moments, but then her voice returned. "What was your name again, dear?" she chirped.

"Virgil, Ma'am," I answered, feeling like a little boy. "Virgil Shepherd. My editor has reserved space for your work in the newspaper. That's a good advertisement for your business."

*300 Words on page 26 or 27. Not the best way to advertise. I hope she won't ask me about that.*

"What a lovely surprise," the old lady bubbled. "When?"

"When would you have time?"

It was silent for a moment on the other end, and I could almost hear her think. At last she said with a chuckle, "Any time, young man. Would tomorrow suit you?"

"That would be lovely, Miss Grey. Will I come to your place, then?"

I could hear her discuss it with somebody else. "How about we meet in the Crystal Grill? Tomorrow, we will be in that part of Calmhaven already, and then we can have a friendly chat while eating a Chef's Salad and drinking a cup of Raspberry tea."

It sounded good. I knew the Crystal Grill. A small, cozy restaurant on the outskirts of town that was overlooking Hanbrook Lake, not too far from Calmhaven's marine.

Perfect. "Shall we say at one o'clock, Miss Grey?"

"One o'clock it shall be," she chirped. "Goodbye Mr. Virgil."

That was it. Done. The conversation was over, and she hung up the phone.

I closed my smart phone as well and leaned against the doorpost of my kitchen. This was almost a sacred moment. I was about to take my first wobbly steps as a journalist, although I could not see how I could write an interesting article in 300 words about an old lady arranging weddings.

But I should not despise the day of small things, and the rest of the afternoon I spent in front of my laptop, churning out questions that could interest the readers of the Sentinel.

Thus, when I arrived the following day at the Crystal Grill, I came prepared.

I was early, something I had done on purpose, so I could choose the best spot and be in control of the interview.

"A table for one?" the waiter, a tall, balding man with huge shoulders and a hawk like nose, asked as soon as I had entered. I stared at the name tag fastened to the lapel of his black jacket. It read *Jean-Pierre.* The man did not look French at all. Rather, he looked like a lumberjack, but he could be Canadian.

"No, I am expecting somebody," I answered while I overlooked the dining area. The place was busy, but at the end, and overlooking the lake, was the perfect spot. "I'll take that one," I said and pointed towards the table.

"Sorry, Sir, that's reserved," the waiter said, forcing a sad grin on his face. "How about here?" He motioned to a table near where we were standing.

Not my idea of a great spot, as it was close by the entrance, but there was not much of an alternative so I nodded, pulled out the chair and sat down. "Just get me a coffee for now," I told the waiter with the French name, and took out my laptop.

At that moment the door opened again, causing a wave of cold air to wash over my back, and a young lady passed by, followed by… an old lady leaning on her walking cane. Jean Pierre seemed to know them as he gave them both a broad smile while he escorted them to the table I had wanted to sit at.

Once there, he pulled out the chair for the old woman and took her coat. The younger lady said something to Jean Pierre that caused him to snort.

*Could it be that the older lady was Miss Grey?*

Her wavy hair with the short curls, was not grey at all, but snowy white. But, she did in fact fit the profile I was expecting: stiff, bent over, leaning on a cane, and her wrinkled face was as least as ancient as Noah's wife must have looked when she walked out of the Arc after the biblical flood.

But who was that lady that accompanied her?

She was about my age, and dressed in fashionable slacks with a fitting, brown jacket and smiled a bubbly smile as she made another remark to Jean Pierre while she pushed her brown pony tail back over her shoulders. An attractive young lady she was, although I didn't care much for the enormous pink glasses perched on her nose.

Then again, my horn-rimmed glasses weren't exactly stylish either.

I studied both women, trying not to stare too obviously, but the more I looked, the more convinced I became the old lady was indeed Miss Grey.

Jean Pierre finished taking their order, and I motioned for him to come.

He arched his brows. "Yes, Sir? Anything else besides coffee?"

"I wanted to ask if you know those two ladies that just came in."

He smiled. "I do. That's Miss Molly Gertrude Grey, and the other woman is her assistant Dora Brightside. They run a dating service slash wedding planner's office here in Calmhaven."

*Bingo. I knew it! It's them.*

"I can recommend their services," Jean Pierre went on. "Two years ago they helped me to find my Winnie." His eyes got a dreamy look as he seemed to peer into happy recollections of the past. "If it wasn't for their help, I would most likely still be a bachelor, watching movies on my lonely couch at night, trying to chase away my despair by eating chips and drinking soda. And..." He lowered his voice and looked around as if to make sure nobody was listening in, "my boss, Alex Pierce, is about to get married and he's also using their services. He and his lovely fiancée are planning an enormous wedding, right here at the Crystal Grill." He raised himself up again and mumbled, "But you probably don't need their help, since you are expecting somebody..." He leaned closer once more, and whispered, "May I give you a suggestion, Sir? For a romantic meal I recommend our Skilled Cod with lemon and capers. Works every time."

"Thank you," I mumbled, not wanting to offend the man. "But I am here on business. In fact, it is Miss Grey I was expecting."

Jean Pierre gave me a knowing smile. "Ah, I see... In that case, I will wish you good luck, and..." he whispered barely audible, "Don't worry, you'll be married in a jiffy."

I had to fight off the temptation to give the man a shove, but instead I closed my laptop and blurted out a stony *thank you* while I pushed my chair away.

"I'll move over to their table," I told Jean Pierre. "You can serve me my coffee over there."

*I was surprised by my own rudeness. I think my nerves were getting the better of me. Sheesh, it's just an old lady from a Bridal shop. Virgil, pull yourself together , man!*

As I neared Molly's table, I felt a rising sense of dread. These were my first steps on my path to become a world famous investigative journalist.

"Miss Grey?" I said, feeling much like that time when, as a boy in first grade, I had been putting chewing gum in Margareta Dolores' hair, and had to explain to mean old Miss Williamson, our teacher, why I had performed that evil deed.

She looked up and our eyes met.

There were small, little lights in her dark blue eyes that, despite her age, sparkled with life and adventure. It was then I realized her wrinkles were not just caused by the years, but it was the smile on her face that had formed some of them. She too, was wearing glasses, although her glasses were at least twice as thick as mine.

"Irvin?" she said. "We've been expecting you."

"Virgil, Ma'am. Virgil Shepherd."

"Ah… of course," Miss Grey wrinkled her nose. "How silly of me. But, never mind. Please sit down young man, so we can have our interview."

No, this lady was not like Miss Williamson. She was as gentle as she was old, and I had nothing to fear. As I pulled out a chair, I knew this would not be very difficult.

## 3

## SOMEBODY GET A MEDIC

**M**iss Grey studied me as I sat down. She may not have gotten my name right, but she struck me as an observant woman. I felt her sharp eyes boring into me as if she could see right through me. But it wasn't unpleasant, and it did not make me feel uncomfortable. Around her there just was no need to pretend. She placed her hand on my arm and said, "Would you like something to eat? Dora and I ordered a Chef's Salad. The treat is on me. The Cozy Bridal will pay for it."

I shook my head, not wanting to abuse the old woman's hospitality. "Thank you, Ma'am, but I am not much of a salad eater. I gave her a weak smile as I opened my laptop again, hoping to start my questions right away. "I am what you call a meat and potatoes man."

"Are you now, dear?" Miss Grey said as she readjusted her glasses. "I heard the hamburgers are rather tasty here. A hamburger maybe?" She tilted her head to the side and looked me straight in the eyes. "And greens are important too, young man. Vegetables, fruits, nuts... that's the stuff that cleans your digestive system. If you don't want to keel over from a heart attack at an early age, you need to put balance in your diet."

There was the twinkle in her eye again as she continued. "Your health is one of the best things you've got, Irwin. Most people don't realize that, when they are your age."

I shrugged. "Virgil, Ma'am. My name is Virgil."

*She's not just gentle and old, but a little irritating as well.*

She frowned. "Forgive me, *Virgil.* Somehow you remind me of my little nephew Irvin, and...," she smiled, "...that's a good thing, for he's a real treasure."

I grinned and nodded politely. "It's nothing, Ma'am. Thank you for the offer, but I am not hungry. I ordered a coffee."

It was then that Miss Grey's assistant spoke up. "Hello," she said, and offered me her hand. "My name is Dora Brightside. I've been helping Miss Molly

Gertrude for quite some years now." Her voice was fresh, almost youthful and had a melodious ring to it. Nice. I liked her. "Virgil Shepherd," I said.

At that moment, Jean Pierre showed up again, carrying a huge tray containing my coffee, two Chef's Salads and two cups of tea.

I closed my laptop again, not trusting the waiter with the tea and the coffee, but he did not spill a drop, and after he had made sure we were all set, he gave Miss Grey a satisfied nod and left again.

Miss Grey turned and asked, "Do you mind if we say a little prayer, Virgil. You know, just to thank God for His goodness. You may even join us if you'd like."

I blushed. "No, Ma'am... you go ahead." I respected religion..., somewhat. It was fine for those who found comfort in it, but I wasn't brought up that way, and had no time for it.

"No problem," she replied in a soft voice. Without further ado, both women bowed their heads, and Miss Brightside whispered a word of thanks to God.

After the prayer, Miss Grey peered at me and placed her hand once more on my arm. "Please call us by our first names. We are Molly Gertrude and Dora. There's no need to be so formal."

I smiled back at her and nodded. "All right, Miss Molly Gertrude, I'll do my best."

Yes, this lady was old, and a little stubborn, but I could not deny she had flair and it confirmed my original thoughts of her being like Aunt Abigail.

She poked around in the salad with her fork, and when she had found what she was looking for, a walnut, she looked up again and said, "Well, Virgil…? Shoot. What do you want to know about the Cozy Bridal Agency?"

I stared at my computer screen and worked my way through the long list of questions while I recorded the whole conversation. Thus I learned that the Cozy Bridal Agency was almost as old as the hills as it had started right after the Civil War in 1870. It was Molly Gertrude's great-great-great-grandmother, Molly White*, who had been a real pioneer, (her name was whispered in reverence) who had understood the need for a trustworthy wedding agency. The Civil War was just over, and the suffering was intense. Husbands were without wives, wives were without husbands, and scores of children lacked either a mother or a father. Thus, Molly White had begun a dating service, and the business had been passed on from generation to generation. It had moved with the times, and moved across the country a few times, but Cozy Bridal seemingly had a long history!

But the present-day Molly, the Molly Gertrude I was interviewing had widened the circle of expertise, and now, besides helping people to find their soul mate, she and Dora were very busy as wedding planners.

And so, both women rambled on and on. It was all very interesting, but I had to confess drowsiness was about to overtake me.

I could think of a thousand subjects that were more exciting than the detailed explanations of how many layers a decent wedding cake should have, and what were the pitfalls of an outside-wedding in the middle of winter. Thus, I felt my eyelids becoming heavier and heavier. Both women were so full of their subject I did not even need to ask any of my questions. They themselves covered the whole scope, as the information just rolled out, and since I was recording everything, I could afford to doze off.

"We've worked together for a long time now," I heard Dora pipe up from somewhere far away.

*Come on Virgil. Wake up.* I sort of shook my head around to shake off the wave of tiredness that threatened to overcome me. Falling asleep during my first interview… That was not a good career move.

"Are you all right, Virgil?" Molly Gertrude asked as she chewed on a carrot.

"Yes… Yes…" I felt my ears getting red. I turned and motioned for Jean Pierre to bring me another coffee. "So… eh…," I mumbled, "… what were you saying?"

Dora frowned. "I said we've been working together for many years now."

"My oh my, time sure flies," Molly Gertrude continued again with enthusiasm. Then a wide grin appeared, and she shook her finger in Dora's face. "Remember that wedding we did with Geraldine Butler and Bob Jones?"

Dora burst out laughing. "Yes, how can I forget? One thing is certain Miss Molly Gertrude, we've made many people happy, and we've seen a lot of satisfied faces."

My eyelids closed again. If I could just lay my head on my arms for a minute… How good would it feel. *Stop it, Virgil. Don't even think about it.*

"Lots of satisfied faces indeed," I heard Molly Gertrude affirm on the fringes of my consciousness, "and a few angry ones, too."

Angry faces?

I shook up. "Did you say *angry faces*?"

Molly Gertrude cocked her brows. "Yes, Irvin... I did."

I was no longer tired, just like that. Angry faces... that was the stuff I was looking for as a journalist. In one of my YouTube courses I had learned that a journalist needed to strike the right balance between the good, the bad and the ugly, and to captivate your readers, it was even advisable to mix in a little more of the bad and the ugly than just the good.

"What do you mean by angry faces?" I asked. "Did you mess up a few times? Were there times when the Country band you hired turned out to be playing Death Metal, or are you referring to a marriage feast, when the wedding cake spoiled and all the guests became sick?"

I felt two pairs of eyes scrutinizing me, and I realized I should have broached the subject with a little more tact.

"Sorry," I mumbled, "I meant—"

"We know what you meant," Molly Gertrude interrupted, "... and don't worry. The answer is simple. We never had such things happening, but yes, some people were not so happy with us."

"Who..., I mean why?"

Molly Gertrude gave me a graceful smile. "Because of my other passion."

"What is your other passion then?" I asked.

"Mystery, young man. Plain, good old mystery. Dora and I love to do our share of amateur sleuthing."

*Bingo. Finally.*

"Do you want to tell me about it?" I urged them, my sleepiness gone.

"Sure," she said with a nod. "Together, we have solved several cases here in Calmhaven, Irvin."

"Virgil, Miss Molly Gertrude. Remember, my name is *Virgil*."

"Of course it is," Molly Gertrude answered. "We've been able to hand over quite a few crooks to the police inspector of Calmhaven, the honorable JJ Barnes."

"And don't forget his deputy, Digby," Dora added. I noticed a small blush appearing on Dora's cheeks.

"That's right," Molly Gertrude continued. "And I can assure you, that the faces of the crooks we caught were not thrilled when they found themselves in prison."

Dora's eyes shone. "I remember how you found out what happened to Abe Mortimer," she laughed. ** And I don't think those crooks you exposed that time when Deborah Smythe went missing were too overjoyed either.

"This is so interesting," I said while I leaned forward. This was the stuff that could put me ahead in my career although I realized all too well I had only 300 words to cover it all.

"Tell me all about it. How are you going about solving these cases, and how come the police didn't catch the crooks, but you did?"

Molly Gertrude was just about to open her mouth, when someone let out a blood-curdling scream, so loud and so terrifying, that the happy chatter of the customers stopped and the pleasant atmosphere of the restaurant turned icy cold and ominous.

All eyes turned to a table on the far end of the room where an older man, dressed in an Armani suit, was clasping his neck with both of his hands while making desperate, raspy and gurgling noises as he was turning blue. He was spitting and spluttering, tottering around until he tumbled to the floor like a great redwood.

Molly Gertrude was the first to react. Despite her age, she jumped up and waved her cane in the air. "A doctor, " she cried. "Is there a doctor here…? Somebody get a medic." Jean Pierre sprang into action too, and ran to the phone to call for an ambulance, but nobody else dared to even move a muscle.

At that moment, the man in the Armani suit slid off his chair and landed on the ground. My heart pounded too. I was clueless as to what I could do. I saw how Molly Gertrude, without a smile this time, shuffled over to the unfortunate man on the floor and ordered another waiter to feel the man's pulse. The waiter's face dropped, and he shook his head.

"The man is dead," I heard Molly Gertrude say, and a wave of consternation washed over the restaurant.

* Read: Get a free copy of The Bridal Train Murder at PureRead.com/cozy-mystery-club

** Read: The Wedding Cake Wipeout

## 4

# MISS MOLLY GERTRUDE'S HUNCH

I jumped up too and walked over to the scene to take a better look at the unfortunate fellow.

He was the first dead person I had ever seen. His face had a strange contorted grimace and an unnatural greenish shine. And although the sight somewhat repulsed me, and I knew I needed to tread carefully, as to not offend anybody, I could not deny the rush of excitement that coursed through my body. After all, I was a budding journalist, and I was there to report on the man's accidental death.

Thus I fished my mobile phone out of my pocket and hoping no one would notice, I took a few pictures. I checked the quality. Not great. In fact most of what I saw were the soles of his shoes and that was not a pretty sight. A fresh sticky glob of red chewing gum, as big as my thumb nail, and several dead leaves were pressed into the rubber, and demanded most of the attention. You could not even properly see the agonized expression on his face. Maybe I could still beef it up in Photoshop. After all, a picture was worth a thousand words, and I only had 300.

I felt a little guilty for acting so heartless, but I pushed the thought out of my system. Wasn't it Henry Grunwald, the famous editor of Time magazine who had said, "Journalism can never be silent. It is its greatest virtue and its greatest fault. It must speak, while the echoes of wonder, the claims of triumph and the signs of horror are still in the air."

"What happened?" I mumbled to Dora Brightside who was now standing next to me.

She pressed her lips together. "Maybe he choked a fishbone," she whispered without taking her eyes off the scene. A crowd of customers had now formed around the dead man's body. Jean Pierre was trying to keep us at a distance.

"Please," he said, "move away. This is not a pleasant sight."

Another man, a young fellow with wavy, blond hair, also dressed in a fine suit, knelt down near the body and again checked the pulse of the unfortunate man again.

"Who is that?" I asked.

"That's Alex Pierce," Molly Gertrude's voice informed me. I turned my head. Molly Gertrude now stood next to us. "Most unfortunate," she added while she shook her head in dismay.

"He's the owner of the Crystal Grill," Dora said. "We know him well, as he and his fiancée, Linda Lane, are about to get married. We are organizing their wedding party." She pulled on my shoulder and nodded toward a pretty, young woman in her early twenties who stood on the side, wringing her hands, a desperate expression on her face. "That's her over there."

"Sure, very interesting…," I said, not paying much attention to such inconsequential details, "… but, who is the man on the floor?"

"That's Albert Gravel," Molly Gertrude replied, having overheard my question to Dora.

*Albert Gravel?* The tycoon, the wealthy businessman, whose controversial statements and actions often

covered the front page of the Calmhaven Sentinel...
That was him?

I knew the businessman wanted to build an enormous water park in Calmhaven, called Water Paradise. One of those gigantic theme parks with slides, rides and all sorts of garish amusements. I had read that Albert Gravel believed his park would draw millions of tourists to Calmhaven. *A boost to the economy* he called it.

But not everyone liked Gravel's ambitions for an uncalm Calmhaven.

Even my boss, Jack Stapleton, hated the idea.

"Imagine what would happen to Calmhaven, Virgil?" Stapleton had said. "Right now we have a wonderful town, with a population of 10,000, and we don't need all that busy confusion from the big cities. As our name suggests, we are a haven of rest, and we want to keep it that way. We have our fair share of tourists already, and they don't come for cheap fairground thrills." He swung his finger in front of my nose, as if I were to blame, and as he spoke I could see the little veins in his neck swelling and becoming rather big. He noticed my concern, as he sneered, "Yes, Virgil, that's right, I am angry. We get enough stressed-out city slickers here already, seeking refuge from their busy lives in our peaceful surroundings. The banks of the Snowy River are among the most beautiful in the country, our pineapple tarts are famous… there's no need for an oversized water park, that will not only boost the economy, but will also steal away our identity. With it will come a wave of crime and confusion. I tell you, the whole idea stinks."

But Albert Gravel didn't care. He was a bully with money, lots of lawyers, and friends in high places, so he had begun to buy up the land…

Molly Gertrude's voice besides me broke through my musings. "For what is your life, it is even a vapor that appears for a little time and then it vanishes away." *

"Excuse me?" I turned and faced Miss Molly Gertrude, who stared at the scene with drooping shoulders. "What did you say?"

"I quoted from the Good Book, Virgil," she said. "There's another fitting story in there, about a rich man whose only goal it was to build bigger storehouses for his wealth, but he died like everybody else, only to find out he had not stored up any riches in heaven." She shook her head in dismay. "Sad, isn't it?"

I nodded, although I wasn't sure what she was talking about. At least she had gotten my name right. I cleared my throat and hoping to say something meaningful, I mumbled. "Very sad. Imagine that, choking to death on a fishbone?"

Molly Gertrude tilted her head and raised her brows. "He didn't choke because of a bone. That wasn't the cause of his death."

"It wasn't?"

Molly Gertrude shook her head. "Look, he had finished his dessert already. He even finished his Devil's Food Cake. There're no fishbones in a piece of fluffy pastry. If he had choked on a fishbone it would have happened much earlier. Nope. Mr. Gravel had completed his meal, and the empty expresso cup indicates that he had finished his meal with a shot of Clamhaven's famous coffee. This was no fish bone, child."

*This lady sure notices small details, but maybe her itchy suspicion bone wane was a little overactive.*

I frowned. "What if a fishbone had gotten stuck in between his molars and had worked its way free…"

Molly Gertrude gave me a weak smile. "That's not likely, Virgil. You may be a talented journalist, but—"

At that instant the front door opened and a massive police officer appeared.

"Meet JJ Barnes," Dora whispered.

I realized I had seen him before. Jack Stapleton had done a TV interview with him once, except I had not been paying much attention to the broadcast, seeing I had to do all the dishes in the office. Thus, I had only followed the broadcast with half an eye. His square shoulders and the muscled arms that stuck out of his short-sleeved uniform gave the impression that he was a seasoned prize-fighter. His square face with the chiseled jawbones, the bristly moustache, and the peering eyes matched the picture.

"He's not as fierce as he looks," Dora whispered again. "If you understand him, and you don't cross him too much, he can be quite a likeable fellow."

When I heard Sheriff Barnes bark out a few orders to a younger deputy with blond curly hair and a boyish face, I wasn't so sure I liked him.

"That's Digby," Dora sang, as she pointed to the young man.

I turned and whispered back, "You mean the deputy?"

Dora nodded and a gentle smile flashed over her face. "Yes," she stated. "That's Digby."

JJ Barnes walked over to the body of Albert Gravel and stared at it for a moment. He shook his head in disgust and then asked in a loud, booming voice, "What has happened here?"

The man in the suit, Alex Pierce, the owner of the restaurant, stepped forward while wringing his hands. "Most unfortunate, Sir," he said in a drooping voice. "He must have had a heart attack."

"Hmm," JJ Barnes grunted and eyed him with suspicion. "And you are…?"

"Alex Pierce, Sir," he said. "I own this place." He raked with his hand through his black hair and wailed, "A heart attack… That's so bad."

"Heart attack?" countered JJ Barnes. "We must let the coroner be the judge of that." He scanned the area and noticed Miss Molly Gertrude and Dora, and his face dropped. "What are you two ladies doing here?" he said. "There's no need for you two to be sleuthing around. As usual, the Calmhaven police force is more than able to handle such unfortunate incidents."

"Good day to you too, Mr. Barnes," Molly Gertrude said in her gentle, crackling voice. "But we were just here. Just a coincidence as we are doing an interview with a reporter from the Calmhaven Sentinel." She pointed to me, something I would have preferred she had not done.

"A journalist?" JJ Barnes licked his lips and smoothed out several wrinkles in his short-sleeved shirt. "Glad to meet you," he said as he stepped forward and grabbed my hand.

Standing eye to eye with the broad-shouldered man made me feel uncomfortable, but I shook his hand with fervor in the hope he would not notice my insecurity.

"Your boss, Jack Stapleton, is a good friend of mine," Barnes continued, still shaking my hand. "Tell him I said hello."

"I will," I mumbled, hoping the man would let go of me.

At last he did, and turned to the crowd who was still standing around, somewhat in shock. In the distance I could hear a siren, and I figured the ambulance and the coroner were coming.

"All right, everybody," JJ Barnes almost shouted it out. "Everyone to their tables. There's no need to be alarmed. We'll take it from here."

But the happy meal was spoiled for everybody. Nobody felt much like going back to their tables, business as usual. Thus, people called for the waiters so they could pay their bill, and the place quickly emptied out before the coroner even arrived.

What was supposed to have been a lovely afternoon in the Crystal Grill had turned into a macabre, unpleasant happening. *Magnificent fodder for sensational reporting!*

"Shall we still finish the interview?" Dora asked me while she pointed back to the table where my laptop was still recording.

I pressed my lips together and shook my head. "We've covered a lot of ground and I think I've got more than enough material." I turned to Molly Gertrude and wanted to thank her for her time, but she appeared to be in deep thought. At last, I heard her mumble to herself, "What if this was not a heart attack, but murder."

I gasped. "A murder? What makes you say that?"

"Shhhh! Keep your voice down," Molly Gertrude urged me. "You don't want to get people all upset. I am not sure, but I have this hunch that things are not as they seem."

"A hunch?" I wrinkled my nose. "That's all?"

"She's usually right," Dora Brightside butted in. "That's what makes us successful in our sleuthing."

"Did you see those thugs outside?" Molly Gertrude asked me in a whisper.

I did not understand what she was talking about. "What thugs?"

"Three of them, armed with clubs," she explained. "While you were staring at the body, I saw them through the window. Scary looking fellows, but then, when they saw JJ Barnes' squad car, they stopped right in their tracks, turned around and disappeared from the scene, as if some man-eating wolf was on their trail."

"You saw all that?" I marveled. "Still, it may not have any relevance to this poor man's death. It looks like a heart attack."

Molly Gertrude nodded. "It does, but don't forget most people wanted this man dead, so we should treat this case with special attention."

"What else could it have been?" I asked.

"Poison," she answered simply. "There are poisons that work in such a way it almost looks like a natural death, and it leaves little trails in the bloodstream."

"I don't know," I said, while I shook my head. "There's not a devil under every stone you encounter."

"You are right, Virgil," Molly Gertrude said, "not under every stone, but some stones have them."

I noticed the man in his suit, the owner, was ashen white. "He sure seems nervous," I mentioned and nodded in his direction.

Molly Gertrude nodded. "We know him well and he's not usually like that. We are in fact organizing his wedding."

I remembered that Jean Pierre had told me his boss was about to get married, but I failed to see Molly Gertrude's point. "Of course, he's nervous," I fired back. "A man has just died in his restaurant. I can imagine better ways of advertising your business."

"It's not that," Molly Gertrude answered me in a gentle voice. "His body language is telling me something else. I will have to find out what it is."

I shivered. What if the old woman was right, and I had just witnessed a murder? Writing an article about a murder was a lot nicer than having to write boring stuff about the great-great-great-grandmother of Molly Grey.

I cleared my throat. "Eh… If you are right, and there is something sleazy going on…," I hesitated, wanting to speak the right words, "… can I report on it?"

"Sure," Molly Gertrude replied as if she was talking about something as simple as changing a light bulb. "You just write a good article about our agency, and we'll keep you posted about this poor man's death."

I couldn't suppress a wide grin. I was beaming. What had looked like a most boring interview was fast turning into a stepping stone to journalistic greatness.

Once we were outside, we had to wait awhile as Molly Gertrude was still talking to someone, but a minute later she came out, looking pleased.

"I talked to the coroner."

"Oh?"

"He said it was a heart attack, clear as day."

I could barely hide my disappointment.

"But," she continued, "I told him he still needed to do some tests on the body, and to look for poison, in particular for Devil's Helmet, also known as Monk's Hood. You see..." in hushed tones she went on, "some poisons are very difficult to detect, even with a blood test, and the symptoms are identical to a heart attack. The coroner didn't think it was necessary. He told me this case was clear, and that he was too busy..." Miss Molly sniggered, "... but I offered him a special batch of Silky Curd cookies if he would look into it." Molly Gertrude's face lit up. "You should have seen his eyes... Did you know Virgil, that the way to a man's heart is through his stomach?"

At that instant, somebody behind us cleared his throat. "Excuse me... what has happened here?"

We all turned and stared in the pale face of a skinny man dressed in oil-stained coveralls. He was wearing a baseball cap, sporting the logo of the Calmhaven Giants, his hands in his pockets, as if he was just taking a stroll.

"Somebody died," Dora explained. "Most unfortunate."

His eyes widened, and he pulled one of his hands out of the coveralls and pushed his cap back on his head. "That's terrible. A heart attack?"

"Possibly," Molly Gertrude said as she eyed the skinny man suspiciously. "And, you are...?"

"Me?" he said, acting surprised by the question. "I am nobody. Just a mechanic. I work for Marlow Messerschmitt, you know... MTC? You must know it... we are the best in town."

"What's MTC?" Dora asked.

The man smiled, revealing a set of not-so-well-kept teeth. "I am surprised you have not heard about MTC. It stands for Messerschmitt Top Cars."

I knew the place. In fact, if my memory served me well, my boss Jack Stapleton had bought his Ferrari there.

"So..." Molly Gertrude asked, "why aren't you in your shop fixing cars?"

The man shrugged. "My boss told me there was a Toyota here with car problems, so I rushed over here. But there's no Toyota here."

"Maybe somebody already fixed it," I said, trying to be helpful.

The man nodded. "Maybe." Then he turned and pointed to a red car parked under a tree on the far-end of the parking lot. "I thought at first it was *that* car. I mean… look at the state of that vehicle. That car has been through the wringer. But…" he pressed his lips and shrugged his shoulders, "… that's not a Toyota but a Pontiac."

All three of us followed his finger, and we saw what the mechanic meant. There, somewhat hidden out of sight stood what once had been a majestic, proud automobile, but had now been reduced to a laughing-stock on four wheels. It looked like somebody had bashed the hood with a baseball bat, and if that had not been enough, poured out a full bucket of purple paint over the top of the car.

"That's what I would call a picture of misery," the mechanic said, shaking his head. Then, he gave us another one of his toothy grins. "Well, I guess I had better go back to the garage." He thought for a moment and then said in a low voice, "So somebody really died here, huh? Terrible."

"It is," I said.

It was almost as if the mechanic wanted to say more, but no words came. He stared at his dirty work boots for a moment and then tipped his baseball cap in a greeting while saying with a slight smile, "I was looking for a restaurant to take my wife out for a romantic dinner, but I suppose the Crystal Grill is not the place to go to. Good day."

"Strange fellow," Molly Gertrude mumbled to herself, after he had turned and walked off.

I glanced at the old lady. She seemed suspicious about just about anything. Then again, I was only a reporter, so it was best to not question her too much.

*James 4:14*

## 5

## IT'S ALL IN THE DETAILS

wo days later my article about the joys of the Cozy Bridal Office was on Jack Stapleton's desk. Well, it was not on his desk, but in his email folder. I managed to keep the article under the required 300 words. I counted 254. And they were 254 Words of pure suffering. If you are not familiar with such things as word count, you may think 300 words is a lot, but believe me, it's just about nothing, especially if you consider I had to wade through almost an hour of excited babble of Miss Molly Gertrude and her assistant Dora. How could I come up with something informative that would hold the reader's attention in only 300 words? As I mailed off my bungling manuscript, I knew it would be rejected.

But that was all right, for I would dazzle Stapleton with an all-exclusive about the murder on Albert Gravel.

For a murder it was!

That much was clear now.

It even said so on the front page of the Sentinel. That morning I had read it myself:


MYSTERIOUS DEATH IN THE CRYSTAL GRILL: ALBERT GRAVEL, WELL KNOWN AS THE TYCOON ABOUT TO BUILD WATER PARADISE

*is believed to have been poisoned during a visit to the lakeside restaurant, The Crystal Grill.*
*Police officer JJ Barnes wishes not to comment for the sake of the investigation,*
*but claims an arrest has been made.*


An arrest had been made?

Who? It was time to contact Molly Gertrude Grey and see what she and her lovely assistant had to say.

I called her on the phone. Molly Gertrude's cheerful voice greeted me.

"Cozy Bridal Office. How may we help you?"

"It's me, Miss Grey, Virgil Shepherd, you know... from the Calmhaven Sentinel. I read there's been an arrest. What's going on?"

It was silent for a moment on the other side, and I figured the old woman had to jog her memory. But she remembered. "Virgil Shepherd," she sang. "How good of you to call. Yes, there's a lot happening. In fact, if you want to come over we'll tell you all about it. If you come over right away, you can join us for a cup of coffee and some of my Silky Citrus Curd Cookies."

Right away? I was scheduled to clean the toilets in the office, but maybe I could say I was on an early lunch and would do them later.

Thus, not even fifteen minutes later I sat in Molly Gertrude's small living room with a cookie in my hand and a steaming cup of coffee before me.

"What's up?" I asked as I dipped part of my cookie in my drink before I stuck it into my mouth.

"It was murder. And as I feared it was Devil's Helmet. The coroner found traces."

I listened in amazement. "Was it in the food?"

"That would be the logical conclusion," Molly Gertrude piped up, "but the tests were inconclusive. The lab found no traces of poison in his food or his drink, but I don't think that excludes the possibility that it may have been something on the restaurant menu that killed Mr. Gravel. They admit that they have no idea how the poison entered his body, but it must have happened right there in the restaurant, as the effects of the poison set in almost immediately. Sheriff Barnes is quite convinced the case it cut a dry."

"He was smoking a lot," I offered as a suggestion. "Could it have been in his tobacco? My boss, Jack Stapleton, told me the man was as unhealthy as a cup of Coca Cola that had been left out of the refrigerator for over a month. He was smoking like a steamboat. Three packets a day."

"No," Dora said rather blunt. "I spoke with some folks that knew him. He stopped smoking, or at least was trying to. He went through all the hoops people go through when they want to give up the habit. You know, anti-smoking band-aids, hypnotism, Nicotine chewing gum, and I think he even tried meditation."

The idea of Gravel trying to meditate was almost comical.

"I see," I said. "I also read that Barnes made an arrest. Who was it?"

"Alex Pierce," Dora replied.

I cocked my brows. "Your friend, that nervous fellow, the owner of the Crystal Grill? You think he did it?"

Both women shook their head. "We don't think so," Molly Gertrude said. "In fact, Linda came to see me, all in tears."

"Linda?" I frowned. "Who is Linda?"

"Linda Lane," Dora added as she wrinkled her nose. "She is his fiancée. We told you earlier."

"Details, Virgil…," Molly Gertrude added. "It's always in the details. As a journalist, you should know that," She was right, of course. It was one of the things that had been stressed on the very first YouTube video about journalism I had watched.

"But why do you think Alex Pierce didn't do it?" I peered at Miss Molly Gertrude, eager to hear what she had to say. "You yourself said his body language was somewhat suspicious. I tell you, if I had done such a dastardly deed as poisoning a man, I would be nervous as hell."

"Watch your words, young man!" Molly Gertrude narrowed her eyes, "There's no need for such colorful language in my house."

"Sorry," I mumbled. I should not forget Molly Gertrude was not from my generation.

"But to answer your question, Virgil," Molly Gertrude went on, "Alex Pierce is a good man. He is not a cold-blooded killer."

*Maybe he's a warm-hearted one.* I thought. The prisons are full of so-called good people.

"You know Albert Gravel wanted to build Water Paradise, right?" Molly Gertrude continued.

I nodded. "Sure, I heard he was buying out small business owners near the waterfront. Most people hated him."

"They did," Molly Gertrude continued. "And the Crystal Grill was no exception. Gravel wanted to flatten the restaurant to the ground."

"Isn't that called *motive*?" I asked.

"It gets even worse," Dora added. "Alex Pierce and Albert Gravel had a terrible fight two nights before the murder. Gravel hoped to force Alex out of the restaurant, but Alex said he would rather die than give up his family business. According to Linda, Gravel then yelled that it could be arranged."

"He said that?" I gasped. In my excitement I swallowed too big a piece of my Silky Citrus Curd Cookie. The wretched chunk disappeared into the wrong throat passage, and I wheezed and sputtered, trying to get air.

Dora ran over and slapped my back. "Easy now, Mr. Shepherd," she said. "One death is enough for the week."

When I had calmed down, Dora gave me a glass of water and I could focus again on the matters at hand.

"What you just said would give Alex Pierce even more reason to kill Gravel..."

"It looks like that, Virgil," Molly Gertrude said. "But journalists and sleuths need to realize that not everything is always as it seems. If you jump to your conclusions too soon, without a careful study of the details, you are apt to make a big mess of things. JJ Barnes came to the same conclusion you just made, and he arrested Alex. But I think he's wrong."

I frowned. "Still it is rather strange, you have to admit. Here is a man who wants to ruin someone's business, even threatens to kill him and then, only two days later, he dies in the restaurant of the man he was fighting with. That can hardly be a coincidence."

Molly Gertrude nodded. "But there's one thing you do not seem to get, Virgil. We know Alex Pierce, and you and JJ Barnes don't. We are even going to the same church. Alex Pierce loves God, and as I already told you, I do not believe, even for a second, that he is a killer."

I did not want to be disrespectful, but I did not agree with Molly Gertrude Grey. "You are biased," I said, trying to sound respectful, but as I heard myself saying it, I knew my raspy voice sounded offensive. Still, there was no other way to say it. "Just because the man believes in the Almighty doesn't make him a saint. The Calmhaven Sentinel almost daily carries reports about weird priests, or strange cults that claim their leader is Jesus Christ himself."

Molly Gertrude stared at me, and for a moment I feared she would ask me to leave. But then, and to my relief, a wide smile appeared. "I am glad to see you have some convictions, young man," she said. "I was almost afraid you were a bit spineless, and although I may not agree with your convictions, I am glad to see we ignited a bit of a spark in you."

*Me...spineless.* I grunted and considered sticking another Silky Citrus Curd cookie in my mouth, just to give me the appearance of being in control, but I didn't. These cookies were not my friends.

"The point is," Miss Molly Gertrude continued, that Dora and I are convinced our friend Alex Pierce has nothing to do with the death of Albert Gravel, and it's our mission to help dear Linda Lane so she and Alex Pierce can get married as was the plan."

I grunted. "Why did Albert Gravel even come to the Crystal Grill if they were such enemies?"

"It's simple," Dora explained. "Because of something Linda told us. You see, Alex figured the best way to overcome an enemy is by making him your friend."

"That's right," Molly Gertrude added. "A soft answer turns away wrath, but a harsh word stirs up anger." *

I stared at them both, not quite understanding what they meant.

"He felt bad about their ruse," Dora explained. "So he invited Albert Gravel to his restaurant. Alex hoped that by showing him he was not vindictive and angry, it would pave the way for a solution."

"And then Albert Gravel died..." I shook my head and could not believe Molly Gertrude and Dora, sweet as they were, could not see what was right before their eyes. Alex Pierce had done it. He somehow poisoned Gravel. He even conspired to invite his enemy in some ruse of reconciliation, and prepared the deadly meal to finish him off. So *what* if the man was a faithful church goer? When a man is cornered it's surprising what depths he will stoop to to protect himself. Molly Gertrude and Dora were sweethearts, but no doubt, they were so full of tart-making, and trying to match people up in their lovey-dovey marriage business, that they failed to understand that reality is raw, ruthless and selfish.

"You don't believe us, do you?" Molly Gertrude said.

I felt my ears getting red. She could see right through me.

"That's all right, Virgil," she continued while she chuckled. "Just let us do the sleuthing, and you do the writing. Before you know it you will have the article you hope to be write, and the truth will be told!" She shook her left index finger in the air, before gathering herself and continuing, "There are *other* suspects too, aren't there, Dora?"

Dora nodded.

"Who?" I wanted to know.

"Well, there're those thugs I saw from the corner of my eyes, those fellows with their baseball bats. And then there's his ex-wife."

"He is married?"

"He was," Molly Gertrude corrected me, "to a rather disgruntled ex-wife, if I am correct. She seems terribly upset by the way Gravel treated her financially."

I squeezed my chin with my fingers. "I didn't know that."

"Details, Virgil, details!" Another chuckle. "We need to check her out too," Molly Gertrude continued, "Maybe she profits from his death? We need to find out."

I frowned. Molly Gertrude's words made sense.

"Yes," Dora added. "and don't forget half the town rather would have rather seen him dead than alive. There were lots of people he was having a beef with."

"So...," Molly Gertrude said in a determined voice as she filled up my cup with more Raspberry tea, "... tomorrow, I'll be going to MTC." As she was pouring she tilted her head and asked, "Would you like to come, Virgil?"

I wrinkled my nose. "Why would you go to Messerschmitt's Top Cars? That's a waste of time."

"Just a hunch," Molly Gertrude spoke. "But you don't have to come. It's up to you."

"No, I'll come," I said in a hurry, afraid she would close the door on her invitation. "It's all in the details, right?"

"Right," Dora said. "And remember the little detail of that bashed up car we saw yesterday?"

"I do," I grinned. "I actually feel sorry for the owner of that car. That vehicle is ruined."

"We know who the owner was," Dora said.

"You do? Who?"

"Albert Gravel. It was his car. I suppose this was not his best week ever."

"Really?" I scratched my head.

"And, it gets better," Molly Gertrude added. "Do you know who sold Gravel that car?"

I cocked my brows, waiting for Molly Gertrude to tell me.

"Marlow Messerschmitt from MTC. There's a definite connection there."

I let out a soft whistle. That was indeed a rather strange coincidence. But what to make of it, I didn't know. Nothing made any sense, at least not to me, but Miss Molly Gertrude seemed to be in her element. She radiated a contagious sense of excitement, and at that moment I understood why she could crack cases that even the police couldn't.

*Proverb 15:1

## 6

# TROUBLE AT THE GARAGE

I had been at MTC once before. Not because I had needed a car, but because nature was calling, and I was forced to make a quick sanitary stop. It turned out, MTC with its wide, glassy windows, right next to its own noisy shop, was the only suitable place around.

I still remembered the massive, sparkling showroom, full of polished cars with doors wide open, hoping to lure potential clients onto the soft, leather seats and entice them to grab the ivory colored steering wheels.

It smelled just as I remembered it. A rich, pleasant smell of rubber, mixed in with the scent of plush car seats hung over the place, and soft classical music made for a relaxed atmosphere.

I wasn't sure what Miss Molly Gertrude expected to find, but it didn't matter to me. I was just observing. The old woman had to carry the torch.

"May I help you? " A tall, slender man in a polyester suit welcomed us with a cheap, plastic smile. His hair was slicked back and as we approached his desk, I could detect the fragrance of his aftershave.

Creed, the same brand my boss, Jack Stapleton, used on his puckered face. But to me, the man rather smelled like Greed. I didn't like him at all.

He cast us another one of his warm, summery smiles, trying to make us feel welcome, in the very same way he had smiled at the thousands of customers who had come before us. "Are you looking for a car?" he asked jubilantly.

"We already have a car," Molly Gertrude said as she offered the man her hand. "We were hoping to speak to your boss."

The man's face darkened. "I *am* the boss. Marlow Messerschmitt." He shook Molly's hand. "Why do you need me?"

"My name is Molly Gertrude Grey," Molly said, as she studied Marlow's face. "And this here is my assistant, Dora Brightside, and this..." she turned to me, "... is a reporter from the Calmhaven Sentinel."

I could tell Marlow was getting uncomfortable as his tongue darted back and forth in his mouth. "All right," he said, trying to sound confident. "Can I offer you some coffee?"

Molly Gertrude shook her head. "Thank you, Sir. This will only take a minute."

"Fine," he said. His smile was gone now and instead, a cold expression had taken its place. "Be quick then. I am busy."

"Have you heard..." Molly Gertrude began, "... of the unfortunate death of the tycoon Albert Gravel?"

"Of course," Marlow said, almost sneering. "It's in all the newspapers, including yours," he cast me an angry glance.

"I was just wondering if you knew Albert Gravel?" Molly went on.

Marlow grinned. "Knowing is a big word. When do you really know somebody? But, yes, I've heard of the man."

"You sold him a car."

"I did?"

Either Marlow was just dumb, which was very unlikely, since he was running a profitable car business, or he was acting dumb. I figured it was the last.

"Yes," Molly Gertrude said. "You sold him a Pontiac Trans Am 6.6. I heard that car came from your place."

I could almost hear Marlow gnashing his teeth. Surely, the man was hiding something, but he kept a straight face. "Maybe," he said at last while smacking his lips. "I sell lots of cars, lady. I don't recall everyone I do business with. What's more, I have a bit of a problem. As a child, I fell off the swing. Landed right on my head and since then I have these amnesia spells."

*How convenient.*

"I am sorry to hear," Miss Molly Gertrude spoke in a soothing voice. "Thankfully, that's why bookkeepers have been invented. You must have a record of your interaction with Mr. Gravel."

I could detect a flash of anger, but Marlow kept his cool. "I do, but I will not let you look at," he said, while he wrinkled his nose. "Who are you anyway, coming in here like that, stealing my time with stupid questions about former clients?"

"Dead former clients," Molly Gertrude corrected him in a firm voice.

"Whatever," Marlow hissed. "I want you to leave. You are not even from the police."

"There's a man in jail who has been charged with murder," Molly Gertrude fired back. "His wife hired us to find out what really happened, and we are planning to do just that."

"Good luck with it then," Marlow said and defiantly waved both of his hands, indicating he was finished. "Goodbye, Miss Grey."

"Thank you for your time, Mister Messerschmitt," Molly said. "Oh, by the way... may I use your facilities. I am sorry to bother you much longer, but I am an old lady, and... well, you know... I have to go more often than you youngsters."

"Whatever," Marlow grunted. "It's over there." He pointed to a door that led into the shop. "Go through that door, the first door to your right says *toilet*."

"Thank you, dear," she mumbled.

I had to chuckle as I was convinced Molly Gertrude didn't consider that man a *dear*, but she was as shrewd as she was old.

It took long, but at last she reappeared again, all smiles and rather chirpy.

"Let's roll, Dora," she said as we walked out. "We've got much to do."

"Are you satisfied," I asked, after I climbed on the back seat. "We did not learn a great deal, did we?"

"We did, Virgil," she spoke mysteriously. "In fact, we learned a great deal. I think we'll have this case cracked before you could say Jack Robinson." She frowned, and turned to Dora who was just taking off, "That is the proper expression, isn't it, Dora?"

"It is, Miss Molly," she said as she began to steer away from the parking.

"There's just a few more loose ends," Molly Gertrude continued. "I was thinking we need to—"

But she could not finish her sentence, as at that moment a loud crashing sound splintered the air, and Dora's car swerved violently to one side and made a full U-turn. It skidded to a halt right near the front door of Marlow Messerschmitt's garage.

Another car had hit us.

"Are you both all right," I cried out to Dora and Molly Gertrude. Dora nodded and Molly Gertrude even managed a smile. "I am like my cat, Misty," she chuckled. "I've got nine lives. I just used one."

When I stared out the window, I saw that another vehicle, a red BMW, had rammed into us from the side. The side mirror on Dora's side was gone, and I imagined the front of the Kia Rio had known better days as well.

Thank God, it appeared no one was hurt.

The driver of the BMW, a middle-aged lady with short, blonde curls and a flimsy red cut out dress, (I noticed immediately her back was bare) climbed out, her eyes as dark as my first cup of coffee in the morning. She had covered her face in thick layers of makeup, and her lips were so red, it almost hurt my eyes. But then, when she opened her mandibles, and a stream of curses rolled out, curses I had not even heard on television, I feared we were in serious trouble. She shook her fist at us while kicking Dora's bumper with her boot. The thing had been so damaged that it came crashing down, barely missing her feet.

"Can't you look where you're going, you dimwits," she yelled. "But you will pay for this. You've ruined my car."

Dora's face paled. "I-I didn't see her. Where did she come from?"

"It's not your fault," I said. "That woman was on the wrong side of the road. It's my guess she roared into the parking area without looking, and just crashed into you."

"I think Virgil is right," Molly Gertrude added, a little pale around the nose herself. "You did nothing wrong."

At that moment Marlow Messerschmitt ran out, and we were amazed by what happened next. He ran up to the lady in the red dress and pulled her into his arms. She burst out crying, which made Messerschmitt unleash a volley of soft kisses on her forehead while he stroked her white curls.

"It must have been his wife," Dora whispered.

At last we heard him say, "Go inside, sweetheart. I'll handle this."

He pulled her towards the door of the garage, and when he had made certain she had left, he turned to us, and motioned for Dora to roll down her window.

"Sorry, we crashed into your wife," Dora bit her lower lip as she stared into the man's face.

"She's not my wife," Messerschmitt corrected. "Just a client, that's all."

A client? What sort of garage was this place?

"But I am very sorry," he continued. "I saw what happened. My client drove way too fast. I'll handle this."

"We need to call the police," Dora said, still a little shaken.

"No police... eh, I mean, there's no need for that," Messerschmitt answered. "It wasn't your fault. Listen, just leave your car here. I'll fix it on my bill, and you come back tomorrow to pick it up."

"Really," Dora asked. "Just like that?"

"Just like that," he gave her a grin. "I sell cars, remember. Fixing cars is what I do. In the meantime, you can have a loaner." He forced a smile on his face and pointed to a Chevrolet that was parked nearby. "There," he said. "The gas tank is full. Take it, no questions asked. Just be back here same time tomorrow."

Dora looked at Molly Gertrude and she looked at me. "W-What do I do, Miss Molly Gertrude?"

The old lady readjusted her glasses and said, "Well, I think we all want to go home. Let's do it."

Thus, only moments later Dora revved the engine of a majestic Chevrolet. The car was just about twice the size of her Kia Rio, but she got it on the road, and we were on our way again, shaken but unharmed.

"What a weird accident," Molly Gertrude mumbled. She turned to Dora and said, "Will you ask your friend Digby to run a check on Messerschmitt? He's hiding something." She thought for a moment and then added, "And ask him if he has any idea who those thugs may have been that I saw on the day Gravel died?"

"Isn't that like looking for the proverbial needle in a haystack? Dora asked. "I mean, you are the only one that saw them. They could have been anybody."

"Not anybody, Dora. These folks were mean. Very mean and very dark. There are not that many people around like that. Such folks have a tendency of being known by the police."

Dora nodded. "Sure, I'll ask him. Anything else?"

"I want to get in touch with Gravel's ex-wife. We need to find out where she lives. I want to talk to her."

⌒

Miss Molly Gertrude was right.

Police deputy Digby had news. The deputy ran a computer search on Marlow Messerschmitt and something rolled out... Gravel and Messerschmitt were involved in a court case. Gravel was suing the owner of MTC, and although Digby could not find out why, it was clear the two men were fierce enemies.

"We are talking millions of Dollars," Digby told Dora over the phone. "Something about a business deal gone sour."

But that was not all. He also had news about those thugs. Right after he and his boss, JJ Barnes had left the scene at the Crystal Grill, they had bumped into three rough-looking fellows.

It had all been a coincidence, Dora explained after her phone call. Barnes had taken the long route back to the police station, a road that led through Walnut Grove, the poor part of town.

And there, as they slowly drove through the street, Digby spotted three fellows with baseball bats.

"Barnes wanted to ask them what they were doing there," Dora told the others, "but they panicked and ran as soon as they saw the police car. A guilty conscience, I suppose. One of them stumbled and fell, and Digby, fast as a jaguar, (Dora said this with shining eyes) caught and arrested him."

She knew his name. Leonel Pike, a small-time crook, and he was still in custody at the police station. "The man fits the vague description you gave," she said as she turned to Molly Gertrude.

Molly Gertrude slapped her hands together, almost as if she had won the lottery. "Wonderful news, Dora," she said. "Why don't you go to the police station and talk to him. They can't hold him for long as he did nothing wrong, so go there right away. In the meantime I'll see if I can track down Albert Gravel's ex-wife."

"Sounds great." Dora grinned.

"And me," I asked. "What will I do?"

Molly Gertrude tilted her head. "You?" She thought for a moment and then replied with a slight smile. "You go where the action is, Virgil. If you want inspiration for your article, it's best you go with Dora to the station."

# 7
## CAUGHT

I posed the question to Molly Gertrude. "I imagine, she is the one who killed him."

Dora was just overtaking a milk truck, and I noticed Molly Gertrude was clenching her jaws. The accident from the day before was still in the forefront of her mind. But when we were back in the right lane, she relaxed and said, "Good thinking, Virgil, and there's more."

She turned to look at me. "Do you know what we saw when we got to her place? "

I had no idea.

"A purple fence," she said while she lifted her finger.

"So?" I had to agree with her that fences should be white, green or brown and not purple, but why was this a big deal?

"It was the same color purple that somebody threw over Albert Gravel's Pontiac." She peered into my eyes and asked, "Remember... his car, parked under that tree?"

I did and tried to make sense of what I'd just heard. "You mean matching, identical, corresponding?"

"That's what I mean, Virgil."

A little smile appeared on Molly Gertrude's face. "The woman was home, and she told us all about it."

"She let you into her house?"

"It wasn't easy at first," Dora chuckled. "When we first arrived, she made quite a stink, but when she realized we were not there to cause trouble, she relaxed, and yes, she invited us."

"We learned a lot about Albert Gravel," Molly Gertrude said. "In fact, once she had calmed down, she was a fairly decent person."

"Yes," Dora agreed, "she even cried, and confessed she was the one that bashed up Albert Gravel's Pontiac."

"It's a long story," Molly Gertrude continued, "and I will spare you most of the details. But Albert Gravel did not treat her well at all. A few days ago he came to her house which, as it turns out, was really his house. He wanted to evict her. "Two weeks dear, and then you need to out." That's when she bashed his Pontiac and threw that bucket of purple paint over the car. She's got quite a temper as we witnessed ourselves, but Gravel just laughed about her actions and told her he would sue her."

"But you don't think she could have killed Gravel? She had all the reason in the world." She had a perfect motive.

Molly Gertrude shook her head. "In all respect to the dear woman, getting the poison into Gravel's body took planning and skill. She is all passion and fury, but this was calculated."

"But do you know who painted her fence?" Questioned Dora. I knew it was rhetorical and she was about to let me in on the secret. "Leonel Pike!"

The greasy bruiser with the baseball bat? Seemingly he was casing the couple and posing as a handyman meant he had access to their house unnoticed."

"Whoa, is he the killer?"

Neither Molly nor Dora said another word.

## 8

# THE PUZZLE PIECES FALL INTO PLACE

When we entered the police station my excitement was rising rapidly. I had only been there once before when I was a kid. My neighborhood friend, little Jack, had convinced me that throwing mud into the hallway of fat Mrs. Steinmetz would be the ultimate thrill, but later that day, when I felt the steely hands of a husky policeman around my neck, and had been hauled off to this very station, I knew little Jack had been lying. The police made me sit in a grungy room for three whole hours, after which my Dad came to pick me up and brought me home where he gave me a belting. I had not forgotten it.

But now I came as an investigator, not as a timid rascal.

Dora explained to a grumpy, bored looking lady with messy hair why we had come, and she paged Digby. Seconds later a door opened and the young man I remembered from the scene in the Crystal Grill stood before us. He seemed overjoyed to see Dora, but his smile froze at once when he spotted me.

He leaned back to scrutinize me a bit better and slipped into police-mode. When I first saw him, I thought he was a likeable fellow, with his boyish grin and blond curls, but now, as I felt his suspicious stare, I realized here was a man that would not hesitate to fine me to the full extent of the law, if he would ever catch me breaking even the smallest of traffic rules.

"Who is that?" he grumbled to Dora, without asking me.

"A journalist from the Calmhaven Sentinel," she giggled. "He's doing an article on the Cozy Bridal Agency."

"I did already," I corrected her, "but now I am doing a second article on Miss Molly Gertrude and Dora's detective work. Pleased to meet you. The name is Virgil Shepherd." I stuck out my hand. Digby hesitated, but then he shook it.

Dora leaned over and whispered something in his ears, but not so soft that I couldn't hear it.

I couldn't help but blush as I heard her say, "Don't worry, Digby. No need to worry, he's a funny little fellow, but he's not my type."

I had to swallow hard. *As if you are my type, Dora Brightside, funny little girl with your silly glasses.*

But, at least Digby's stance softened somewhat. He nodded, and his smile returned. "All right," he said, "you both are in luck. JJ Barnes just left the office and he won't be back for another hour. That Leonel Pike is a nasty fellow, but who knows, maybe he'll talk to you."

Digby led us into the dumpy, dark area where they held the more undesirable characters of Calmhaven until they could be processed to a more suitable place, and pointed to a holding cell near the end of the hallway.

Leonel Pike may have been a lovely baby when he was first born, but much of his original beauty had faded because of his life on the street. The slender fellow with his greasy hair and deep-seated hardened eyes was not a man I would want to meet on a lonely highway on a Saturday after midnight.

But after Dora had introduced herself and had assured him she was not connected to the police, he seemed eager to talk.

"What makes you think we were at the Crystal Grill?" he asked after Dora had posed the question to him.

"We saw three fellows with clubs there," Dora answered. "But then they ran. We thought you may have been one of them."

"What if I was?"

"Were you?" Dora asked. "You did not break the law, so there's no harm in telling us if you were."

He let out a sneer. "Somebody beat us to it."

"Excuse me?"

"Somebody already did the job for us."

"What job?" Dora asked.

"We wanted to give him a warning. But we didn't need to anymore."

"Warning? I am not sure if I follow you." Dora's eyes widened.

Another sneer. "Sometimes we work for Giovanni. He needs guys to settle scores. Always in exchange for a few Benjamins, of course."

"Benjamins?"

He scowled, as if he could not understand our ignorance. "Money. Dollars. Bacon. We are the score settlers, although we do nothing serious, like harming people. Nothing illegal."

"Who is Giovanni?"

"Giovanni Toscanini. He runs the Casino in Boulder Valley. A lot of folks try to cheat him, and that fellow who just died was no exception. Giovanni told us to send him a message."

"You mean… Albert Gravel?" Dora frowned.

Pike grinned. "Yeah, him. He owed Giovanni money, but he didn't want to pay. But we had nothing to do with his death. We were just going to remodel that fellow's car, but we were too late. Somebody had already done that." He grinned as he thought back on that day. "Whoever messed up that Pontiac, did a better job than we could have ever done. They even doused that car in weird, purple paint."

Dora shook her head and readjusted her glasses. Then she turned to Digby. "We need to add Giovanni Toscanini to the list of suspects."

Pike overheard her and laughed out loud. "Nah… Giovanni is not a killer," he snorted. "This Gravel fellow was a regular customer to the casino, and he owed Giovanni some serious cash. Killing the goose that lays the golden eggs is never a great idea."

"So, that's it?" Dora asked. "Anything else, Mr. Pike?"

"Nope," Pike said. "What else do you want me to say, little lady…? I mean," he snorted, "I wouldn't mind having a beer with you. Fancy a date?"

Dora gave him a weak smile. "No. thank you Mr. Pike. And… if I may say so, there are other career paths available for you. Ever considered getting a real job?"

Pike burst out into a cackling laugh. "You sound just like my mother, baby. You are just as naive as you are pretty—"

"—That's enough," Digby interrupted, and he banged on the bars with his club. "Respect from the likes of you couldn't do any harm, Pike."

Leonel scowled at Digby. His look made me shudder as I could almost feel the crook's anger and I was happy we could leave the station.

The next morning, just as I was buttering my toast at the breakfast table, my mobile phone rang. I looked at the screen. *Dora Brightside.*

"Hello Dora, Virgil here. What's up?"

"Can you come over, Virgil? Miss Molly Gertrude thinks we have a breakthrough."

A flash of excitement rushed through my veins, but how could I not to go to my work at the Sentinel. "I would love to come, Dora... but I've got a lot of work at the office..."

It was silent for a moment, but then Dora piped up, "With what, Virgil? Cleaning toilets and serving out donuts?" I could hear her sigh. "But, it's fine with me," she continued. "It's just that Miss Molly Gertrude thought you would be interested for the sake of your article."

"I am," I howled, while my mind slipped into fast gear. If I could just come up with a great article, Jack Stapleton wouldn't mind it if I skipped pouring bleach in the toilets for one day, and donuts weren't good anyway for the oversized office personnel.

"I am coming, Dora," I said at last. "Go nowhere without me."

Half an hour later I was sitting again on the backseat of the loaner, wondering where we would be going. "We'll explain it all to you on the way," Dora had said. "Just hop in."

"On the way where?"

"We are going to Messerschmitt, to pick up my Kia Rio—"

"—And," Miss Molly Gertrude butted in, "—solve the case." She turned to Dora and asked, "You did call JJ Barnes and Digby, did you?"

Dora nodded. "Just as you asked, Miss Molly. They expect us there in half an hour. Barnes was a bit miffed you were nosing in on his case again though, Miss Molly." Molly just chuckled.

As Dora steered the car out of Molly Gertrude's street, the old woman filled me in on what Dora had called a breakthrough.

"Virgil," she began, "I think we solved the mystery."

"You mean," I said with hesitation, "you know who killed Albert Gravel?"

She nodded. "I think I do." Then she told me what she had discovered. "After you went home yesterday, Dora, and I drove to the place of Albert Gravel's ex-wife."

"She was home?"

"She sure was," Dora answered without taking her eyes off the road.

"And do you know what we found out?"

I shrugged my shoulders. "No... what?"

"Albert Gravel's ex-wife is the same woman that crashed into our car yesterday." Molly Gertrude said.

I felt a shiver up my spine. The angry woman that kicked the bumper off Dora's car was Albert Gravel's ex-wife. Would she have killed him?"

## 9

## ALL THE DUCKS IN A ROW

At that instant the MTC came into sight. The place looked dreary and dark, as if someone had thrown a blanket of horror over the place, and I wasn't sure anymore if I wanted to come along.

Molly Gertrude noticed my hesitation. "Come on, Virgil… A journalist dares to go where angels fear to tread."

I swallowed hard and followed.

Messerschmitt was at his usual station by the desk and was reading the newspaper.

"Ah," he said with his sales-smile, "… there's the mystery crew. If you'd all be men, I'd call you the Hardy boys." He laughed heartily about his own joke and stepped away from his desk. "The Kia Rio is all yours," he grinned. "I think my workers are just checking the air in the tires."

"We are not only here for the car." Molly Gertrude said. "There's another pressing matter."

"There is?" he frowned. "What may that be?"

"The customer you were so concerned about, the lady who smashed my car. She's been taken into custody for the murder of her husband, and she's asking you to come. She insists she didn't do it, and that you can vouch for her whereabouts at the time of the murder."

Marlow looked shaken, but quickly gathered himself.

"How long will this take, old lady? I'm a busy man."

"Not long, dear, but Sheriff Barnes insists you come, and I would vouch if you refuse it may look a lot like you are obstructing justice. We believe it was someone else, but it's important that you and Mrs. Gravel clear your names so we can finally wrap this nasty mystery up, don't you think?"

Marlow Messerschmitt grinned a sly smile, and nodded, pulling on his jacket.

"Maybe you can take this car, and we will jump in my Kia?" said Dora, "We will meet you at the station."

Soon they were back on the road and heading to a meeting with JJ Barnes, and more than a few suspects. Among them, the killer!


In the station Barnes growled as the fur walked in. He was not happy to have some rookie reporter sticking his nose in police matters, and even less so that Molly and Dora were sleuthing their way into is business. He did have to admit that the old girl had compelling evidence, and if for nothing other than curiosity he wanted as much as anyone else to see how the Gravel case would unravel.

Alex Pierce sat cuffed. Beside him, Leonel Pike, also cuffed and scowling. A somewhat disheveled Mathilda sat on then opposite wall, gripping her handbag tightly. Marlow glanced across at her and began to make his way across to take the seat beside her, but Deputy Digby ushered him into a seat beside the other two suspects.

I could see Molly Gertrude eye each person carefully as she took the center of the room. In between the men and Mrs. Gravel, Barnes stood with his arms crossed, daring anyone to make a wrong move. I took a seat beside Mrs. Gravel, praying the steely eye of Branes would not land upon me.

"Alex," Molly began, "You had every motive and perfect opportunity to finish off your nemesis with that meal you gave him!" Alex sat up startled that Mrs. Grey, his churchgoing friend, would hurl such an accusation. Alex began to protest his innocence, and Barnes sharply reprimanded him, reminding him that anything he said not only could, but certainly would be used in evidence against him if he did not shut up.

"It is suspicious, Alex, that you would invite Albert Gravel, only days after threatening one another, to come and eat at your establishment. The very establishment he was threatening to raze to the ground!"

All eyes were on the squirming restaurant owner. I couldn't help but see the guilt crawling all over him. Molly had this chap bang to rights. I knew the killer was hiding behind a cloak of piety and now it was clear.

"But you didn't do it," Molly said matter of factly, "not a trace of the poison was found in the food or drink that you served."

I felt somewhat disappointed, but the train of accusation didn't stop there. Once she was on a roll, Miss. Molly didn't miss a beat.

"Not so for you Mr. Pike! You told us that you had no job, is that right? Except of course your work for Giovanni Toscanini? But a little bird told us you do some handy man work on the side?"

"There's no law against a man earning an honest crust!" Pike protested. "Anyways, what's that got to do with Gravel?" Pike's shifty eyes darted from Molly to Barnes to Mrs. Gravel and back again.

Then, in a sudden shift of attention, Molly spun around on her rickety legs and pointed straight at the owner of MCT. "Marlow, were you with Gravel's ex-wife, Mathilda, at the time of the murder?"

"Yes, yes, I was," he nodded furiously. "Can we go now, I've got work to do?"

"Sir, you are as wicked as you are cunning!" said Molly Gertrude, "I disliked you from the moment we walked into your garage." Marlow simply stared back. What did he care what a foolish old woman thought of him.

"Marlow Messerschmitt, I believe you killed Albert Gravel," she stated, without blinking an eye.

For a moment it looked as if the world stopped.

There was absolute silence for just a second and Messerschmitt's hand, which was just lifted in the air, stayed there motionless as if frozen. Then he dropped both of his hands and stared at her with big round eyes that slowly seemed to turn black.

"You've got no proof," he hissed.

"Still you did it," Molly Gertrude said undeterred. "Gravel was about to win a court case against you. It would have ruined you. Your relationship with Mathilda was more than a working one, and you knew all the ins and outs of Albert Gravel. Little did she know the information she shared with you could ruin your life, and you figured it was time to act."

"How dare you!" Messerschmitt scowled. "My private life is nothing to do with you, and that court case would have been overturned. Anyways, I wasn't even there when that scoundrel died." Marlow pointed to Alex, "he's the one that poisoned the food! I never set foot in that deadly restaurant."

"That is one thing that you have said that's true, Mr. Messerschmitt, "But you have been to Albert Gravel's car," Molly Gertrude continued, "You sold him the car, and knowing his gambling addiction from Mathilda, I vouch that you kept a spare key just in case Gravel missed his payments and you wanted to retrieve the vehicle. I believe you injected poison into his nicotine chewing gum that he kept in the glove compartment of the car. You used Devil's Helmet, a poison that is hard to detect, and thus you made it look like a heart attack. But it was cold blooded murder."

"You are crazy," Messerschmitt fumed. "You've got no proof I was even near his car."

"Yes, I do," Molly Gertrude answered. "The other day when I went to your bathroom, I noticed your locker. There are several lockers, but this one had your name on it, and since you had failed to lock it I took the liberty to look inside."

"That's illegal." Messerschmitt clenched his fists and looked like a tiger ready to pounce on his prey. "I will sue you so bad, old woman, that they will have to carry you out to the poor house when I am done with you."

"No, you won't," Molly Gertrude answered. "It is you that will be carried out, only you won't be going to the poor house, but to the Federal Prison. In your locker I found your coveralls, the ones you wear when you are working on cars. They were all stained with purple paint, the paint that Mathilda had dumped over the car. You must have rubbed your sleeves over it when you entered the vehicle."

"That's ridiculous," Messerschmitt roared. "I wore those coveralls when I was painting Mathilda's fence together with her."

"No you didn't. Mathilda told me that Mr. Pike here had kindly offered to repaint the fence any color of her choosing, courtesy of Toscanini, for all of the business Albert Gravel brought to the casino. But there's more. How do you explain that little vial of poison I found in your locker too? Or did you plan to use that to remove spilled paint on Mathilda's nails or something?"

"All lies," he hissed. "I will sue you. You've got no proof."

But Molly Gertrude continued undeterred. "You somehow knew he was dining in the Crystal Grill, and he would likely eat one of his gums after the meal, so you told your mechanic there was a broken Toyota at the parking lot of the Crystal Grill, just so he could check for you if your evil little plan had worked."

"Stop it... Everybody back!"

Suddenly Mathilda leapt from her chair. I cringed, as I knew that voice. It had the same angry tone I had heard the day before after the car crash. Everyone turned around and stared in the contorted, angry face of Gravel's ex-wife, Mathilda. Her hands trembled... she was holding a gun that she had whipped from her handbag.

"Albert almost ruined my life," she yelled, "but he's gone. Now, leave me and Marlow alone, so we can still make something out of our lives." I could see it wasn't only her hand that trembled, but her lip was too. "I will not let you take Marlow away from me... Not over my dead body," she continued.

"Lower the gun, Mathilda." Molly Gertrude's voice was calm, almost kind. "Do not make matters worse. At this moment you have done nothing wrong... not yet."

I marveled. Where did that old lady got her strength from? I was shaking in my boots.

"You have no real proof," Mathilda howled. "I know Marlow. He would never do such a thing." She turned to Messerschmitt. "Right honey-bird, tell them you are no killer."

But honey-bird didn't answer her. He just stood there with a defiant, stony face.

It made Mathilda even more nervous as she looked with wide, fearful eyes at Molly Gertrude again. "If you promise to drop the whole matter, and forget everything you found, you can walk out of here... alive."

Molly Gertrude shook her head. "It doesn't work that way," she answered in a low voice."

"Y-You are bluffing," Mathilda mumbled, but I could see she was just about to lose it. By now, I was about as nervous as Mathilda. Tears began to roll down her face and shaking like a leaf in the wind she dropped the gun to the floor.

Thank God. It was over.

Messerschmitt knew it too.

This was his last chance. He let out a guttural roar and in one amazing jump that would have made any athlete competing for the Olympic gold medal jealous, he leapt from the room, smashing the door closed behind him. Without hesitation, JJ Barnes set off in hot pursuit, lumbering after the desperate killer.

Alarm, confusion and pain were fighting for dominance on Mathilda's face as she stared at the door that Messerschmitt had slammed shut, back to us, and then back to the door again. At last, she let out an agonizing cry and burst out in tears.

"Now, now, dear," Molly Gertrude coaxed her. She walked over the woman, picked up the gun from the floor, placed it carefully in Deputy Digby's hands and took Mathilda in her arms, pressing the weeping woman to her chest.

I sat there stunned. I was certain Sheriff Barnes would catch Marlow Messerschmitt, but was not going to hang around to find out.

That day, I did not go back to Molly Gertrude's house for Raspberry tea. I had a job to do, and I locked myself in my room and wrote my first real article for the Calmhaven Sentinel. I called it: "The day Albert Gravel died," I smiled when I was done, exhausted, but satisfied.

7000 Words. I wondered if maybe I had overdone it.

# EPILOGUE

A s I expected, they soon caught Messerschmitt. They finally arrested him on Boulder Valley International Airport the following day, and he gave a full confession. He had to. Just as Molly Gertrude had said, they found tiny injection marks on the chewing gums in Gravel's car and he was ultimately sentenced to twenty years in the Federal Prison. Good riddance to bad rubbish.

JJ Barnes released Alex Pierce that evening, and the next week, right on schedule, he and Linda Lane got married in the Crystal Grill.

I was there as the official journalist for the Calmhaven Sentinel. Jack Stapleton had heard about my help in the investigation and told me he was impressed. "Maybe we've got a better position for you," he beamed. True to his word, I no longer had to clean toilets or do other such menial jobs. He promoted me to write stories about the Bingo evening in the local old-folks home, and I was even allowed to report about stolen bicycles.

And my article about Albert Barnes? It was never published. "Way too long," Stapleton explained. "I'll take care of it." And that was it. The only mention in the Calmhaven Sentinel about the whole thing was a small article by Jack Stapleton himself, that stated that JJ Barnes solved a very difficult case, and that the people of Calmhaven could rest assured that their enthusiastic police force was watching over them, even in their sleep.

So I quit.

I decided journalism wasn't my calling. I am now going for higher mountains.

Now, I will be a writer. A real good one too. Maybe I'll even write a mystery or two.

And Miss Molly Gertrude and Dora?

To be frank, I am not that fond of Raspberry tea, and I always seem to choke on her cookies. But I must confess, I may need Molly's Cozy Bridal agency before too long myself, as I met a gorgeous young woman. Her name is Patsy, and she is talking about getting hitched.

So, if we ever decide to step into that sacred little gondola called marriage, I think I know just the ones to organize the party!

THANK YOU FOR CHOOSING A PUREREAD BOOK!

We hope you enjoyed the story, and as a way to thank you for choosing PureRead we'd like to send you this free Special Edition Cozy, and other fun reader rewards...

Click Here to download your free Cozy Mystery
PureRead.com/cozy

**Thanks again for reading.**

See you soon!

If you loved this story why not continue straight away with other books in the series?

Wedding Cake Wipeout

The Bridal Dress Disaster

A Fishy Murder Most Foul

The Mystery of the Missing Bride

Missing Cash and the Corpse in a Cabin

The Dead Man's Stolen Book

# OR READ THE COMPLETE BOXSET!

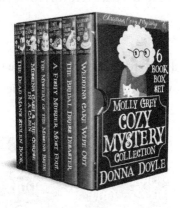

**Start Reading On Amazon Now**

OUR GIFT TO YOU

AS A WAY TO SAY THANK YOU WE WOULD
LOVE TO SEND YOU THIS SPECIAL EDITION
COZY MYSTERY FREE OF CHARGE.

**Our Reader List is 100% FREE**

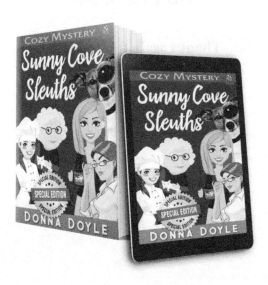

Click Here to download your free Cozy Mystery
**PureRead.com/cozy**

At PureRead we publish books you can trust. Great tales without smut or swearing, but with all of the mystery and romance you expect from a great story.

Be the first to know when we release new books, take part in our fun competitions, and get surprise free books in your inbox by signing up to our Reader list.

**As a thank you you'll receive this exclusive Special Edition Cozy available only to our subscribers...**

Click Here to download your free Cozy Mystery
**PureRead.com/cozy**

**Thanks again for reading.**
See you soon!